Hello!

My name is Hans. Welcome to my story.

You might know me from some of your favorite stories: "The Little Mermaid," "The Princess and the Pea," or "The Ugly Duckling."

My full name is Hans Christian. But you can call me H.C. That's what my friends call me. Plus, if we shorten my name to "H.C.," we'll have more room to write our adventure.

I am a teller of stories, specifically of fairy tales. And have I got a story for you.

I was born in Odense, Denmark, on April 2, 1805. The city is southwest of Denmark's capital, Copenhagen.

When I was young, I received a magic hat. When I put my hat on my head, I am transported to marvelous places with marvelous people. Well, for the most part. There have been some not-so-marvelous people.

But every story needs a villain.

I invite you to join me on my adventures.

So grab a hat—a baseball cap, a cowboy hat, one of those hats with a tiny propeller on top! If you don't have a hat, just use your imagination. You'll be using it a lot.

P.S. If you're wondering what part of this adventure comes from my imagination and what part comes from the real world, read "The H.C. Chronicles" at the back.

GRAB YOUR
HAT
AND GET
READY FOR
AN ADVENTURE!

In 1812, Napoleon and his great army of 691,000 soldiers marched on Moscow...

In the frozen city, fires broke out. The French soldiers beat a hasty retreat through one of the harshest Russian winters.

Only 90,000 of his men made it out of the terrible Russian campaign alive.

Rumors of the defeat spread rapidly. Fearing nationalist attacks and rebellions, Napoleon sent his soldiers to enlist new recruits.

In Denmark, H.C. Andersen's father was recruited.

However, during his journey to France, he fell ill. He was sent back to Odense.

But recruitment was not enough, so soldiers started kidnapping people.

④

My father had often talked about Napoleon's great army. He told me that it needed men and that he was planning to enlist.

I don't want to go to war, especially not like this!

Let me go! I don't want to go to war!

If you try to run away again, I'll tie you up until we reach Paris!

I didn't want to be tied up...

...but I certainly didn't want to go to war. I wanted to go home!

I want to go home!

Hey! Wait!

???

Be quiet! You'll make them angry.

How did we end up here?

I don't know about you, but I enlisted.

I don't care! Don't try to stop me!

Get in the bag!

It's not fair!

Ow!

What's in the bag?

A little brat! Keep an eye on him.

With that pounding rain and the watchful guards, anything I tried was doomed to fail!

No problem!

I spent the following days in the back of the wagon. They fed me a few crumbs and drops of water.

I decided to escape as soon as I could, but the opportunity never came up. Instead, I listened to the soldiers talk about their lives.

I have no idea how much time I spent in that coach, but it felt like an eternity.

BLABLABLA

Bonjour!

Welcome to Paris!

Isle Louvier, Célestins, Grand Arsenal

⑦

Fit for service.
No good.
Fit! Fit! Fit!

What's this?

???

BLE BLE BLE

Catch him! Nobody mocks the uniform and gets away with it!

RUN!

All right, where were we?

What?!?

He, he!

Where did you find them? A town dump?

...well...

No excuses, get rid of him.

There's no place for you here.

Ha!

Wait! You can't just abandon me here.

They weren't listening. They were only concerned with collecting soldiers for their dear Napoleon.

I was alone in Paris...
without money, food, or anyone to understand me.

Place de Grève

???

What's changed?
You still don't
have money, food,
or anyone who
understands you!

Victor!

You missed the
beginning.

So what?
It won't
kill me!

I'm already dead. That must
have been some beginning!

HAHAHA

I brought a friend.
Allow me to introduce
Edith Piaf.

Bonjour!

Bonjour!

We just got to
the part where
H.C. was expelled
from the army.

Sir, yes
sir!

Ha! Okay, let
me continue.

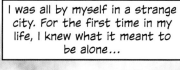

I was all by myself in a strange
city. For the first time in my
life, I knew what it meant to
be alone...

How will I get
back to Denmark?
To my parents?
To Karen?

Pont Neuf and La Samaritaine

Quiet, stomach!

BROOUMBLE

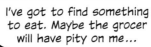

I've got to find something to eat. Maybe the grocer will have pity on me...

I've always striven to behave honorably and stick to my principles. As I'm sure you can imagine, preparing to commit my first crime was no picnic...

Get out of here, you rascal!

I'd never thought that I could one day become a thief, but hunger can make you do many things.

You look as starved as I do.

I'm thinking the same thing. But how...?

11

???

The police!

Stop in the name of the law!

TRiiii

Hurry, boys! It's Javert!

Who?

He's the meanest of them all!

You can say that again!

Ha! Gotcha!

Let me go!

I didn't do anything!

BLONK!

?

You... you've killed him...

Grr...

WAAAAH!?!?!

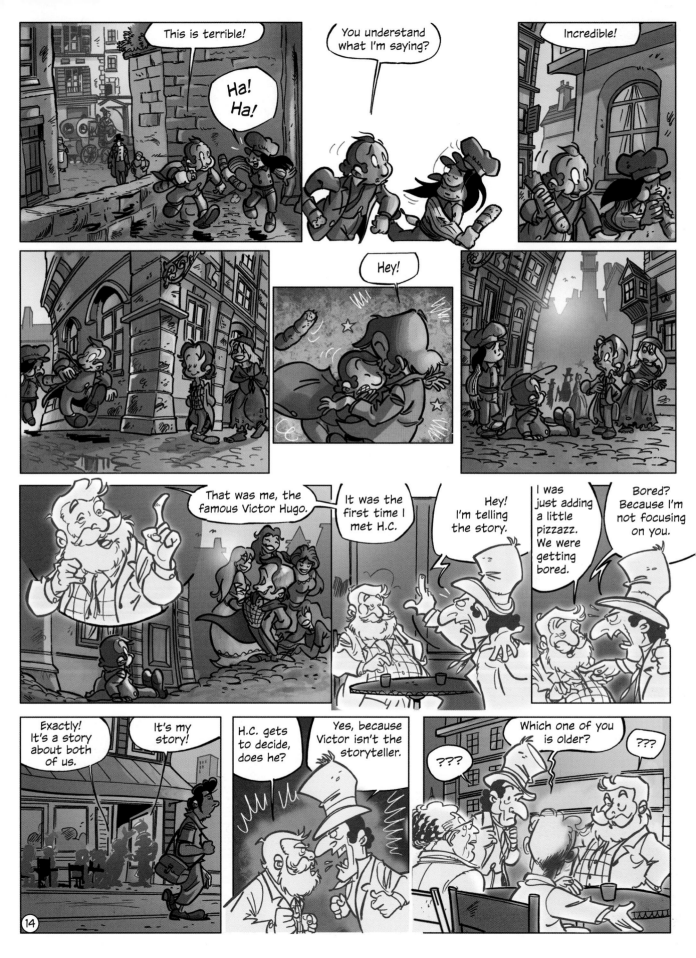

Sorry, friends!

We'll stop arguing.

I was born in 1802.

And I was born in 1805. I was 8 or 9 when we met.

Then I was 11 or 12. But I seemed much more mature.

Ha! Ha! Ha!

Mature just means boring!

Enough. Where were we?

HA HA HA

Can't you be more careful?

Excuse me!

My name is Cosette. Are you Parisian?

No, I'm from Denmark!

Welcome!

What are you doing here? In beautiful Paris?

My name is H.C. I was kidnapped by soldiers who wanted to enlist me in the army, but I'm too small. They tossed me into the street as soon as we got here.

That's really sad. It's terrible that they are making children go to war.

You seem too angry to be dismissed, like you want to fight.

???

Tons of people want to enlist. But the army doesn't want them.

Victor's father is a captain.

He probably threw you out of the barracks.

Tell me more.

I've been living in the street for years. Victor helps me from time to time...

I come from a wealthy family. They don't want me to hang out on the street. But it's more fun here. If you want adventure, it's the perfect place.

This is a nightmare, not an adventure.

Only if you choose that mindset.

You listen to me! I've had my share of adventures.

Can you tell them to me?

Not so long ago, I could create them. But I can't anymore.

How strange! What happened?

I had a magic hat that I could use to travel to my imagination, but it was taken away.

I never had a magic hat, and that never stopped me.

Victor tells wonderful stories. He can show you how.

It's very simple: you just use your surroundings.

That soldier over there could be fun!

Hurry!

Uh... I don't want to...

Relax, H.C. You'll like it.

Excuse me, I just caught this boy who confessed to running away from the army. There's a reward for bringing back a deserter.

What?!?

You've done France quite the service!

Whaaaat?!?

Off to prison!

Nooooooooo!!!

16

Ha! Ha! Ha!

???

It was a joke, H.C. Meet Paul.

Sorry, kid!

He's one of my father's men. A real prankster!

Only joking, young man.

Well it wasn't funny!

Sorry.

Yes it was!

Hee hee!

Ha!

HAHAHA

You can come sleep at the house. You don't have a place to stay.

Thanks! Plus, I'm getting hungry.

Rue du Dragon

You can share our bread. There is enough.

How kind! Thank you.

The house is wonderful. It's old, amazing, and where the orphans live.

You're no orphan.

No, but I love going there. I find the best audience for my stories!

Sounds great!

And it's good training for me to become a writer! That's my dream. I'll be a great writer, maybe the greatest of them all!

Write much?

All the time! But getting published is hard.

Why?

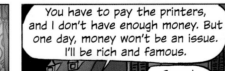

You have to pay the printers, and I don't have enough money. But one day, money won't be an issue. I'll be rich and famous.

Sounds hard!

Yes. But just you wait... One day, they'll beg me on their knees for the opportunity to publish me.

Here we are!

17

Welcome to the orphanage.

Magnificent! You live here?

I don't, but let's go in! We're always welcome.

Can you imagine, asking the great Victor Hugo to pay to publish?

Are you ok? Wake up!

What? Where am I?

You were chasing some kids. You must have tripped.

Yes, I remember! Thief!

Don't worry! The kids might have been starving.

Let them starve. There's no law against that!

But...

They're criminals. They must be punished! Especially after attacking me.

They're only children. A little dry bread won't ruin me!

Theft is theft! And I'll make sure they spend the rest of their lives wearing a ball and chain!

You're not going to hunt them down for a bit of bread, are you?

Of course I am. Without me, this city would be anarchy.

Are you okay?

Uh, sorry. We're just talking about justice.

Drop your pathetic excuses, I don't have the time!

VLAM!

After I catch that scoundrel, I'll stick him in prison.

Not bad, Javert... Not bad at all!

WANTED

How did you make this long journey?

Oh yes! I bet it's a great story!

Well it all started on a cold and rainy day...

I told them how I got to France and about my trip on the wagon...

...and then we ran into you all.

That's quite a sad story.

Yes, it's tragic. But you also talked about a magic hat and the stories that you lived.

It's true! It gave me the ability to enter my own stories. It saved my life more than once. But when I think about it, I don't know if it was a blessing or a curse...

Why's that?

I became addicted to it! I forgot how to use my imagination. The hat did it for me.

How about that!

When I lost my hat, I also lost my imagination. The worst thing is that I know I'll never have those same kinds of experiences again.

I don't need a hat! I do quite well for myself without a silly magic hat!

It's true, but you can't judge if you haven't tried it.

Maybe I should show you how I do it. It could be fun. I also had all kinds of adventures!

Oh yes, good idea! You should try it, H.C.!

Listen...

One day, I met the most beautiful girl. She danced so well that she enchanted everyone.

After hypnotizing men, she stole their money.

???

20

And when she was caught by the police, I helped her escape and we hid in Notre-Dame.

Notre-Dame?

Yes, it's a cathedral in Paris. But let me finish...

We were cornered...

Then a rope appeared, and we grabbed it...

We were pulled up into the air with great force. Who was our mysterious rescuer?

When we reached the top of the cathedral...

We met an unusual person.

He had been in love with the girl for a long time. He admired her from his tower. The man was deformed. His face and body were completely contorted, and he had a gigantic hump on his back.

He had seen Javert chasing us.

Javert! He was also after you?

Javert is real. We know that too well, but the others are purely imaginary. The hunchback and the girl don't exist, but they helped me anyway.

How did you get pulled up to the top if they didn't exist?

There's no explanation. It's fantasy!

That happened with my hat.

What's the line between reality and fantasy?

KLONG! KLONG!

I didn't see the time pass. I have to go!

See you, H.C.!

Bye! I'll come back as soon as I can!

She looks like she's in a rush.

She never tells us where she goes. Every time we ask, she is very vague and mysterious.

Cosette reminds me of a pretty girl at home.

You think... that Cosette is pretty?

Well, yes. Don't you think so?

Now that you mention it, maybe...

Does H.C. like Cosette?

The way you use your imagination is strange! It reminds me of what I was like with my hat.

POP!

I can show you how I do it if you like!

You think you could teach me to control my imagination?

It's not control. You just have to externalize it. Maybe that's your problem.

What?

Don't try to control it. Instead, try to relax.

What do I do?

Here's an idea: I tell you a story and you listen.

Ready?

Let's do it.

It's time to start looking beyond things. What's in my hand?

??

A broom?

Yes. But what do you see?

Hmmm, it could be a cane!

It's a cane, and I can't walk without it.

After being shot in the leg, I was unable to walk.

Does it hurt???

Sitting helps.

Climb on!

24

Ha! Ha! Thank you, but we're here today for you to join the ranks of the musketeers. It's an honor!

Oh!

BLOM

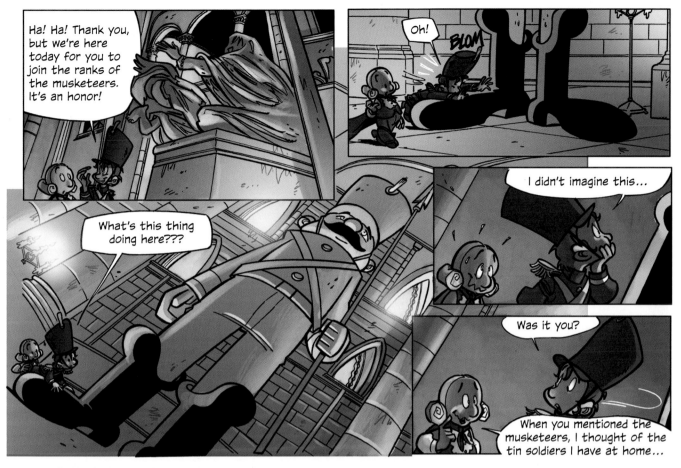

What's this thing doing here???

I didn't imagine this...

Was it you?

When you mentioned the musketeers, I thought of the tin soldiers I have at home...

POP!

POP

POP!

POP

This is a disaster!

I've brought others along in my stories, but nobody's been able to influence them like you...

I'm sorry. Are you angry?

Can you do it again? Make a gargoyle.

Huh? What's that?

They're ugly, grinning statues that drain water from the roofs of some buildings.

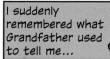
I suddenly remembered what Grandfather used to tell me...

Your imagination doesn't come from a magic hat, it comes from inside you.

Ok, I'll try!

Gargoyle??? Gargoyle!!!

KWIIIIIII
KRIIIIIIIIII
BIIIIGGG

DZIIIING

KWAAWW

26

KWAAAKK!

GROWWW!

Quack.
Ha! Ha! Ha!

Grumpf.
Ha! Ha! Ha!

Now that's really weird...

...

Victor, tell us a story, pretty please?

28

Victor, tell us a story!

It...

was fantastic!

I've never had so much fun. We should do it again!

Yes! I never knew it could be so much fun without the hat!

Victor, tell us an adventure! Please?

True. I've just returned from a fantastic story. I'll tell you the whole thing. But first, I want to introduce you to Hans Christian.

You promised!

Hello, Hans Christian!

Just call me H.C.!

Ok, H.C.!

H.C. is very special. Like me, he's a storyteller.

Ha! Don't exaggerate.

Not at all. If we're lucky, he'll tell us one later...

We'd prefer you.

Then it shall be me.

Once upon a time, there lived a man named Valjean, Jean Valjean.

Jean Valjean was very special: he was born with a pure heart. He couldn't stand to see others suffer.

29

He'd rather die of hunger than see them starve. He gave money to the poor.

Above all, he loved his wife. Unfortunately, this couple couldn't have children.

Their house was too big for just two people. Every night, they thought about all the love they could give to a child.

Jean knew a child needed loving parents.

If only I had parents like that...

Wait! I DO have a mother and father!

?? ?? ?

Hey, what's up?

What? I was telling a story!

I want to go back to Denmark! I have to find a way to get back home.

If you tell a story, I promise to help you get back, ok?

It isn't a good time. I'm not sure I can!

Concentrate. And then I'll find a solution to your problem.

...

Ok, I'll try.

Long ago...

there was a porcelain emperor who ruled over a vast country. He could obtain whatever he wanted with a snap of his fingers.

TCHAA!

Being made of porcelain, he had very sensitive ears...

He loved song, but there was no voice in all his empire sweet enough for him.

LALALA!

He had heard that the sweetest and most beautiful voice in the land was that of the nightingale. But where could he find such a bird?

He sent his soldiers in search of it, and it wasn't long before fortune smiled on him.

A lucky soldier chanced upon a shepherdess who owned a nightingale. But this bird only sang for one person: a chimney sweep, who was the sweetheart of the shepherdess.

It was a picky bird.

Cosette? How strange!

The emperor offered her gold, but she only wanted to give the nightingale to the person she loved.

Furious, the emperor shut the shepherdess up in the tower of the palace.

The nightingale was finally his... but it didn't sing a single note.

When the chimney sweep learned that his sweetheart was a prisoner, he went to the emperor and demanded she be released immediately.

The chimney sweep assured him that the nightingale would only sing for him.

But the emperor didn't want to hear it. Either the bird sang for him, or the shepherdess would remain in the tower forever.

The chimney sweep knew that the nightingale would never sing for the emperor, but he was clever, and caught a crow.

He painted it to look like a nightingale. Then he tied a ribbon around its beak and brought it to the emperor.

When the emperor saw the chimney sweep's bird, he was impressed. It was twice as big as his own, so it must sing twice as well.

In exchange for the crow, the chimney sweep demanded the release of the shepherdess, which was granted at once. As soon as they were free, the two sweethearts fled as far as possible from the palace...

The emperor carefully removed the ribbon from the beak of the bird, which immediately unleashed a caw so terrible... that the porcelain flew into pieces!

KRAOOOO

That's enough! Stop!

What's going on, Victor?

Why should he stop?

It's a waste of time. Nothing is happening!

I think you're jealous!

You're jealous!

Was it too good?

I am not! Be quiet!

HA HA HA

Hey! Look: there's a reward of five francs on his head.

We just have to turn him in to Javert!

What?!? We won't do that!

But we could buy clothes and food.

34

How can I put this... I had never felt such jealousy before! And I was only 12 years old!

And what's this about Cosette?

H.C. opened my eyes. I didn't realize that I felt that way.

But you'd known her for a while.

Yes! But H.C. made me realize my feelings. Outsiders can do that.

It's true!

Yes, yes!

Yes!

In the days that followed, my relationship with Victor became tense. There were posters all over town... what publicity!

All the children knew me, and they wanted my autograph on the posters.

It was strange to become famous for being wanted by the police. But nobody turned me in.

BLOF!

You little rascal!

Hmm... H.C. Andersen?

Ha! Now I even have his name!

And you, mind your own business!

Hey, what's going on with you?

Be quiet, H.C.!

We should go after Cosette, not fight!

You're right, but what can we do? I can't fix her problems.

Yes, but we can help her forget them. Let's take her on an adventure!

That's it!

I'm sorry I hurt your feelings, Cosette.

Thank you. I appreciate it.

Would you like to join our story?

What if Cosette loves H.C.'s story?

How can I split them up? Let's wait and see, maybe it's all in my imagination...

What's going on? Why am I reacting like this?

But why do they have to be so close?

Victor?

Maybe I should embarrass H.C....

Victor!

Huh? What?

Don't start without us!

I wasn't!

H.C. is bugging me.

Ready?

I have an idea! Let's go!

YOINK!

Oh no!

Oh my!

WAAAAA

Was that you?

What? Of course not!

The princess is gone!

Who is on the crow?

The frog prince! He's is trying to take the princess away.

We can't just run after him!

TiiiiF

Storks!

They can take us to Cosette!

Let's get her!

Oops, sorry Victor!

We're back!

I was so scared. I thought we were going to be stuck there forever.

But how?

Maybe the slap?

You're right.

Tell me if you want another. I have to hurry now. See you later!

Kiss!

What a girl!

I have to get rid of H.C. before Cosette falls for him...

If I turned him in, Cosette wouldn't see him anymore...

Are you okay?

Yes, let's go back to the orphanage, it's getting late.

Good idea. We need our rest after that story.

He just wants to go home. And he's nice, isn't he?

But if I get the reward, I could get my stories published and get rid of him...

Maybe even buy Cosette a dress or locket. She would be so happy!

44

Where have you been?

Leave us alone! Go away!

You don't love me?

No! I am in love with Victor, my sweet Victor!

Daydreaming again, are you?

POP

Yes...

He even has to ruin everything in my dreams.

I have something important to do. Bye.

Where should we meet?

Marché des Innocents

At the orphanage.

Hmm, how can I help?

I know where he's hiding.

You see?
I told you he was there.

???

Cosette?

Cosette! Wait!

La Force Prison

If ever I needed my magic hat, now is the time...

I'm so happy that I caught you.
And don't think you can escape.
There is no way of getting out of here.

Ha! Ha!
Bye,
H.C.!

CLAP CLAC

There she is!

47

She lives here?

She has a home?

Cosette! I have to tell her the truth.

???

What do you want? Did you bring your friend Javert with you?

Forgive me.

You betrayed H.C.! You need to apologize.

But I did it for you!

For me? You've lost your mind.

I don't feel like myself anymore...

You need to get help.

Yes, but... I think I love you.

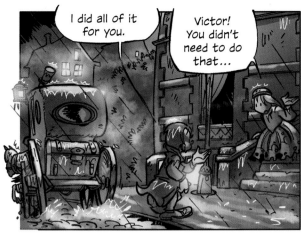

I did all of it for you.

Victor! You didn't need to do that...

I also have feelings for you!

I thought you liked H.C.! That's what drove me crazy with jealousy. I hope you can forgive me.

If you want me to forgive you, you have to help me free him.

Do you really live here?

Yes. My parents are rich, but I dress up so the other kids don't find out...

Rich or poor, it's all the same to me. I love you just as you are, Cosette!

What about H.C.?

Let's go get him.

Let's go find Gavroche. He could help us.

Do you have any ideas?

We must distract the guards.

But how?

???

BOM

BOM

Z

49

Who's there?

Good try!

TLAST
FLAS

UURRGHHH!

Ha! Ha! Ha!
Come catch me!

You monster!

I think he's gone.

I'll keep
a lookout.

Here are the keys
for H.C.'s cell.

KLIK
KLANK

H.C.! Are you there?

Victor? You came!

Quiet! You'll wake the other prisoners. I'm here to rescue you.

What if you get locked up?

I'd deserve it...

What?

Nothing. Hurry up before we're spotted.

You need to get out of the country. If not, Javert will hunt you down for the rest of your life!

What should we do?

We'll go to the stagecoach stop, you might have some luck there.

What?

Now all you have to do is buy a ticket.

But I don't have any money! If I did, we wouldn't be here in the first place.

Here! That should be enough to get you to Denmark.

Where did you get this money?

It's not important. Think of it as a gift, for all you've taught me.

I can't accept this! I could never pay all of it back!

That's okay!

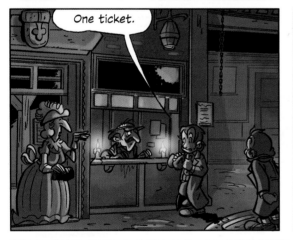

One ticket.

Here you are, young man. It's that coach over there.

Here's your ticket.

This is the nicest thing anyone's ever done.

Thank you.

When will you come back to tell us stories?

I won't, not while you have a storyteller like Victor!

You're lucky to have him! He'll be one of France's great writers one day. Who knows, maybe the greatest!

To Denmark?

Yes!

Thank you, H.C. You're a real friend.

We'll miss you!

I'll miss all of you!

Bye!

You can talk?

See you, H.C.!

Goodbye, Victor!

Bye!

Look out, here comes Javert!

???

I've almost got him! Give me a hand!

Where did they run off to?

???

BLONK

Ouch!

Where are they?

Just wait 'til I get my hands on them!

What the...

???

I miss H.C.

We'll see him soon!

Bye!
See you again!

Wow, I really like traveling.

To travel is to live!

The thought of seeing my parents again warmed my heart. A soft breeze caressed my face, and I quickly fell asleep.

After a few days, we arrived at Odense. It was a great relief to finally be back home.

I am sure!

Yes. But I would do it again in a heartbeat.

That was a very sad story.

Yes. Nevertheless, I don't regret anything. Nothing at all!

You learned about yourself.

Yes! I made new friends. And I learned to use my imagination and that I didn't need my hat anymore.

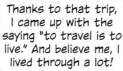

Thanks to that trip, I came up with the saying "to travel is to live." And believe me, I lived through a lot!

That'll be 162 euros, please!

I don't really have any money. Does anybody?

Run!

THE H.C. CHRONICLES

When my grandfather first gave me my magical hat, I thought I needed to wear it to be imaginative. I thought my funny cap was the portal through which to see mermaids and soldiers and castles. But as I learned from a mysterious monk, my imagination was inside me the whole time.

Victor reinforced this idea.

I did not dream up Victor or other people and places in this book. I did not summon them like I did with my ugly duckling.

Keep reading to see who's who and what's what. And be sure to keep your ears and eyes open. You'll never know who or what will inspire you.

VICTOR HUGO

Victor Hugo (1802-1885) was a French author who loved to write about ordinary people. His stories weren't about castles, ballerinas, and mermaids. He focused on the suffering of people. My story "The Little Match Girl" focuses on suffering, too. He thought so much about French commoners' misery that he wrote an entire book about it. It's called *Les Misérables,* or *The Miserable Ones.*

WHO'S WHO

Did you recognize any of my fellow ghosts? We had a wonderful time in the City of Light. I was having fun riding bikes along the Seine when, suddenly, Eiffel.

AGATHA CHRISTIE

Agatha Christie (1890-1976) was an English writer of detective stories. She was known for her clever plots. She was the best detective writer the world had ever seen.

EDITH PIAF

Edith Piaf (1915-1963) was a French singer. I absolutely adore her…even though I met her for the first time about 50 pages ago. Her most famous song is called "La Vie en Rose." That translates to "Life in Pink."

DR. SEUSS

Dr. Seuss (1904-1991) was a master of nonsense. You might know some his books: *The Cat in the Hat, The Lorax,* and *Horton Hears a Who!* He made the most marvelous drawings.

DANNY KAYE

Danny Kaye (1913-1987) was a comedian, singer, and actor. He played me in the 1952 movie about my life. He was known for his lively pantomimes. To pantomime means to act without words.

EDGAR ALLAN POE

You might have recognized my friend Edgar Allan Poe (1809-1849) by his iconic mustache. He was an American poet, short-story writer, and literary critic. He is very famous for a poem called "The Raven."

VICTOR HUGO AND LES MISÉRABLES

The main character in *Les Misérables* is a man named Jean Valjean. He is a peasant who goes to prison for stealing bread to feed his sister's starving family. You might remember that I stole bread in this book. Stealing is not good.

When I stole the bread, I was really, really hungry—so hungry that I thought I might not be able to go on. Was it right for me to steal the bread when I thought I might starve? Should I have gone hungry and kept my honor? Jean Valjean asked himself these questions. Victor Hugo dedicated his life to writing about morality and how we treat others. I think we should treat others as well as we would like to be treated. And I don't plan to steal again…even as a ghost!

THE HUNCHBACK OF NOTRE DAME AND THE CATHEDRAL OF NOTRE DAME

The Hunchback of Notre Dame is another famous novel by Victor Hugo. The story takes place during the 1400's in Paris. It centers around Quasimodo, a deformed bell ringer, and his unrequited love for a dancer called Esméralda. You may have seen them earlier.

Another key character is the cathedral itself. You can see it on the cover of this book—and in real life if you go to Paris.

The Cathedral of Notre Dame—pronounced like noh truh DAHM—stands in the center of Paris. It was built from 1163 to 1250. One reason it might have taken so long is because it featured an architectural innovation: *flying buttresses* (arched supports on the outside of the building). The buttresses strengthen the walls and the large stained-glass windows. The windows allow light to enter the building and make it look as if you're looking into a kaleidoscope.

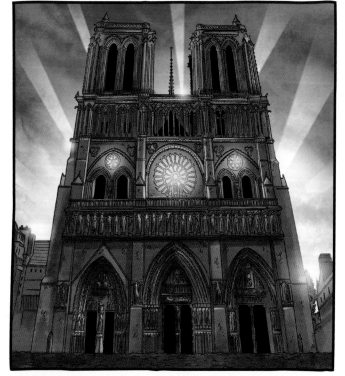

In 2019 a devastating fire broke out in the cathedral. Sadly, much of the roof was destroyed and the central spire collapsed in flames. Thankfully though, the main structure survived, and the French people plan to rebuild their historic symbol of Paris.

THE NIGHTINGALE

I wrote a fairy tale very similar to the story I told my French friends. It is about an emperor and the most beautiful thing he ever heard.

A nightingale had an uncommonly beautiful voice. But it had a very common appearance: it was a small, gray bird. When the emperor first heard the nightingale sing, he was entranced. At once, he ordered that the bird have the finest treatment at his palace. He was to sing to the emperor whenever he was asked.

One day, the emperor received a package. It was a glorious mechanical nightingale. The bird was covered in silver and gold, sapphires and rubies. The mechanical nightingale sang a song just as beautiful as the real nightingale. The emperor had the mechanical nightingale sing and sing its one song. The real nightingale flew far, far away.

The emperor gave the mechanical nightingale the royal treatment. For over a year, the bird delighted the emperor and his court. It continued to sing, until the day it didn't. Its mechanics were worn.

Years passed, and the emperor grew ill. As he lay in his golden bed, he heard a beautiful song. It was the real nightingale! The bird continued to sing until the emperor was better. Of course the emperor wanted the bird to stay at the palace. But the nightingale wanted to bring joy to everyone, not just royalty. The emperor understood, and the nightingale flew away singing.

Created and illustrated by
Thierry Capezzone

Written by
Jan Rybka

Directed by Tom Evans
Designed by Brenda Tropinski
Illustration colored by Feeloo
The H.C. Chronicles written by Madeline King
Photo edited by Rosalia Bledsoe
Proofread by Nathalie Strassheim
Manufacturing led by Anne Fritzinger

World Book, Inc.
180 North LaSalle Street, Suite 900
Chicago, Illinois 60601
USA

For information about other World Book print and digital publications, please go to
www.worldbook.com or call 1-800-WORLDBK (967-5325).

For information about sales to schools and libraries,
call 1-800-975-3250 (United States) or 1-800-837-5365 (Canada).

Library of Congress Cataloging-in-Publication Data for this volume has been applied for.

The Adventures of Young H.C. Andersen
ISBN: 978-0-7166-0958-2 (set, hc.)

The Adventures of Young H.C. Andersen and His Friend Victor
ISBN: 978-0-7166-0963-6 (hc.)

Also available as:
ISBN: 978-0-7166-0968-1 (e-book)

Printed in the United States of America
by CG Book Printers, North Mankato, Minnesota
1st printing March 2020

Photo credits: Dutch National Archives: 60 (Joop van Bilsen/Anefo);
© Getty Images: 60 (Roger Viollet), (Betty Galella); Public Domain: 61;
© RKO Radio Pictures: 60; © Shutterstock: 59 (Lorelyn Medina), (Aqua),
60-61 (dinvector), 61 (Everett Historical).

WORLD
BOOK
www.worldbook.com

Museets rekonstruktion af kuglepostens under en køretur i 1956.